The Three Sillies

Holt, Rinehart and Winston ❊ *New York/Chicago/San Francisco*

The Three Sillies

A folk tale illustrated by Margot Zemach

/Published simultaneously in Canada by Holt, Rinehart and Winston of Canada, Limited./Library of Congress Catalog Card Number: 63-14413/Printed in the United States of America/99857-0113/

ONCE UPON A TIME there was a farmer and his wife who had one daughter, and she was courted by a young man. Every day he used to come and see her, and stop for supper at the farmhouse; and the daughter used to be sent down into the cellar to draw the beer for supper.

One evening she had gone down to draw the beer, and she happened to look up at the ceiling; and she saw an axe stuck in one of the beams. It must have been there a long time, but somehow or other she had never noticed it before; and it set her to thinking.

She thought it was very dangerous to have that axe there, and she said to herself, "Suppose he and I were to be married, and we had a son, and he grew up to be a man, and came down into the cellar to draw the beer, and the axe were to fall on his head, what a dreadful thing it would be!"

And she put down the candle and the jug, and sat down and began crying.

Well, they began to wonder upstairs why she was so long drawing the beer, so her mother went down to look after her and found her sitting there and the beer running over the floor.

"Why, whatever is the matter?" said her mother.

"Oh, Mother!" said she. "Look at that horrid axe! Suppose we were to be married, and had a son and he grew up and came down to the cellar to draw the beer, and the axe were to fall on his head, what a dreadful thing it would be!"

"Dear, dear! What a dreadful thing it would be!" said the mother, and she sat down by her daughter and started crying, too.

Then, after a bit, the father began to wonder what was keeping them so long; and he went down into the cellar to look after them himself. There sat the two of them crying, and the beer running all over the floor.

"Whatever is the matter?" said he.

"Why," said the mother, "look at that horrid axe! Just suppose, if our daughter and her sweetheart were to be married and have a son, and he grew up and came down into the cellar to draw the beer, and the axe were to fall on his head, what a dreadful thing it would be!"

"Dear, dear, dear! So it would!" said the father, and he sat down beside them and started crying.

Now, the young man got tired of waiting up in the kitchen by himself, and at last he went down into the cellar, too. There sat the three of them crying, side by side, and the beer running all over the floor. He ran over and turned off the tap.

Then he said, "Whatever are the three of you doing, sitting there crying and letting the beer run all over the floor?"

"Oh," said the father, "look at that horrid axe! Suppose you and our daughter were to be married and had a son, and he grew up and came down into the cellar to draw the beer, and the axe were to fall on his head!"

And then the three of them started crying worse than before.

But the young man burst out laughing, and reached up and pulled out the axe.

And then he said, "I've traveled many miles, and I've never met three such big sillies as you three before. Now I shall start out on my travels again. When I can find three bigger sillies than you three, *then* I'll come back and marry your daughter."

So he wished them good-bye and started off on his travels, and left them all crying because the girl had lost her sweetheart.

He set out, and he traveled a long way, and at last he came to a woman's cottage that had some grass growing on the roof. The woman was trying to get her cow to go up a ladder to the grass, and the poor thing would not go. So the young man asked the woman what she was doing.

"Why, look" she said, "look at all that beautiful grass. I'm going to get the cow onto the roof to eat it. She'll be quite safe up there, for I shall tie a rope around her and pass it down the chimney, and tie the other end to my wrist. Then she can't fall off without my knowing it."

"Oh, you poor silly!" said the young man. "Why don't you cut the grass and throw it down to the cow?"

But the woman thought it easier to get the cow up the ladder than to get the grass down to the cow. So she pushed her and coaxed her and got her up, and tied a rope around her and passed it down the chimney, and fastened it to her own wrist.

The young man went on his way, but he hadn't gone far when the cow tumbled off the roof and hung by the rope in mid-air. The weight of the cow pulled the woman up the chimney, and she stuck fast.

Well, that was *one* big silly.

And the young man went on and on. He stopped overnight at an inn, and they were so full at the inn that they had to put him in a room with another traveler. The other man was a very pleasant fellow, and they got very friendly together.

But in the morning, when they were both getting up, the young man was surprised to see the other hang his trousers on the knobs of the chest of drawers, and run across the room and try to jump into them. He tried over and over again, and couldn't manage it; and the young man wondered what he was doing it for.

At last the stranger stopped to wipe his face with a handkerchief.

"Oh, dear," he said, "I do think trousers are the most awkward kind of clothes. I wonder who could have invented such things. It takes me the best part of an hour to get into mine every morning, and I get so hot! How do you manage yours?"

So the young man burst out laughing, and showed him how to put them on. And he was very much obliged to the young man and said he never thought of doing it that way.

So that was a *second* big silly.

Then, the young man went on his travels again. And he came to a village, and outside the village there was a pond, and around the pond was a crowd of people. They were reaching into the pond with rakes and brooms and pitchforks. The young man asked what was the matter.

"Why," they said, "matter enough! Moon has tumbled into the pond, and we can't fetch it out!"

So the young man laughed, and told them to look up into the sky, and that it was only a reflection of the moon in the water. But they refused to listen to him, and abused him shamefully; and he got away as quickly as he could.

So there were a good many sillies bigger than those three sillies at home. So the young man turned back home again, and married the farmer's daughter; and they lived happily forever after.